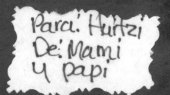

by
Nadia Krilanovich

Moon Child

Illustrations by
Elizabeth Sayles

TRICYCLE PRESS
Berkeley

Library of Congress Cataloging-in-Publication Data

Krilanovich, Nadia.
 Moon child / by Nadia Krilanovich ; illustrations by Elizabeth Sayles. — 1st ed.
  p. cm.
 Summary: Animals interact with the moon on the horizon.
 [1. Moon—Fiction. 2. Bedtime—Fiction.] I. Sayles, Elizabeth, ill. II. Title.
 PZ7.K8964Moo 2010
 [E]—dc22

                          2009032304

 ISBN 978-1-58246-325-4 (hardcover)
 ISBN 978-1-58246-366-7 (Gibraltar lib. bdg.)

Printed in China

Design by Betsy Stromberg
Typeset in Proforma and Goudy Sans
The illustrations in this book were rendered in pastels and acrylics.

1 2 3 4 5 6 — 15 14 13 12 11 10

First Edition

To my family, who always believed
—N.K.

For Jahmair, a star not far from the moon
—E.S.

When I curl up tight,
I fit into the moon.

I bring my knees to my chest and point my toes,
until I am tiny and round, moon-sized.

I smile at the twinkling stars,
and whisper softly, *hello moon*.

I am a moon child.

I can balance the moon
on the tip of my nose.

I can pinch the moon between my fingers,
and pluck it from the sky.

When I stretch out my arms,
I circle the moon in a big hug.

I snuggle in my cozy bed,
soft and warm.

Stars sing lullabies

as the moon watches over me.

Sweet dreams,
moon child.